My Snowman, Paul

Written by **Yossi Lapid**

Illustrated by **Joanna Pasek**

ISBN 978-0-9973899-0-6

To Susan,
Without your love and
support, this book series
would not have been
possible.

It was a snowy winter day

And I was in a mood to play.

So mother said, "Hey listen Dan,
Go build yourself a nice snowman."

"I don't know, Mom, it's getting late,
And snowmen aren't all that great.
In fact, Bill says they're just plain snow..."

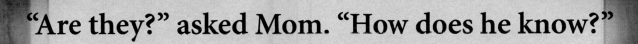

"Are they?" asked Mom. "How does he know?"

"All right," I said, "so let me try..."

And, soon, my snowman stood up high.
'Cause it was awesome, I must say,
How well the snow packed on that day.

I had great fun for quite a while...

But then I saw Bill's mocking smile...

I felt like having a quick snack...
But then this voice snapped: "Hey,

How dare you think of gingerbread
When I'm still waiting for my head?"

I was amazed by what I heard,
I couldn't say another word,
I patched together head and all
And he said: "Hi!

My name is Paul!"

So I said: "Hi, my name is Dan...
Now, what's this all about, Snowman?"

"Well," answered Paul, "I'm here to play!"

"Too bad," I said. "You cannot stay!
Bill, over there, is watching us..."

"Indeed," said Paul. "But what's the fuss?
We simply want to have some fun!
How can that bother anyone?
No, I don't care about this Bill...

C'mon, I'll race you up that hill!"

"What fun!" I said, "What's next, Snowman?"
"Well," answered Paul, "Let's make a plan!"

Then we shook hands and hugged and all
And, now my new best friend is Paul.

Dear Reader,

Thank you for reading
My Snowman, Paul!

If you like this book, please
take a moment to post
a review on Amazon.

Your support makes a big difference, and
helps other readers discover and enjoy
Snowman Paul's exciting and humorous
adventures.

Visit my website, lapidchildrensbooks.com
to learn about new books, special offers
and occasional newsletters.

And if you sign up for the mailing list, you
will receive a special FREE GIFT from
Snowman Paul!

In gratitude,
Yossi

Made in the USA
Middletown, DE
03 December 2020